Please Bear's Birthday
is an original concept by
© Diana Mather, Avril Lethbridge
& Mary-Ann Mackenzie.

Author Copyright © Diana Mather,
Avril Lethbridge
& Mary-Ann Mackenzie.

Illustrated by Mary-Ann Mackenzie

A CIP catalogue record for this book
is available from the British Library.

Maverick Arts Publishing Ltd
Studio 4 Hardham Mill Park
Hardham Pulborough
West Sussex RH20 1LA
+44 (0) 179887 5980

PUBLISHED BY MAVERICK ARTS
PUBLISHING LTD
© Maverick Arts Publishing Limited
May 2011

ISBN 978-1-84886-067-4

Please Bear's Birthday

A NICE BEAR NAUGHTY BEAR STORY

NICE BEARS
NAUGHTY BEARS

There are nice bears and naughty bears
Shy bears and haughty bears

Messy bears, oh what a sight
And bears that always think they're right

Bully bears that have no friends
And kind bears that make amends

Pushing, shoving, grumpy bears
Not bothering to see who cares

But you and I know bears that say
Please and thank you every day

And soon all bears are bound to find
Life is nicer when you're kind.

 Please Bear

Please Bear is very busy, as busy as can be
He's writing invitations for his special birthday tea.

"Please come to my party – it really will be fun
With silly games and lots of food to share with everyone."

Thank You Bear

Thank You Bear is quick to say, "I'd love to come and play
And many thanks for asking me to share your special day."

He counts up all the money that he has got to spend
Then off he goes to buy a special present for his friend.

All the Bears

Soon Please Bear's friends are on their way
Keen as mustard to come and play.

A party with friends is always great
Let's hurry, we must not be late.

Shy Bear

But feeling really, really small
Shy bear stops outside the hall.

"Oh dear, I'm feeling very shy
I know I must try not to cry."

Kind Bear

"Now please don't worry," says Kind Bear
Who has been watching from the stair.

"Take my paw, we'll go and play.
I'll be beside you all the way."

Sharing Bear

Sharing Bear, who's kind and clever,
Calls "Come with me, let's play together."

When playing games we must take turns
That's something a nice bear learns.

Boasting Bear

Boasting Bear shouts "Just watch me!
I will win, you wait and see."

But boasting comes before a fall
And whoops, she really is no good at all.

Helpful Bear

Helpful Bear helps where she's able

Till all the food is on the table.

"There's plenty for everyone you'll find,"

Says Mummy Bear who's always kind.

Table Manners Bear

It's time for tea. Hip Hip Hooray!

Time to eat...Not time to play.

Remember to sit as well as you're able

And keep your elbows off the table.

Greedy Bear

One bear's plate is piled too high
"STOP, Greedy Bear!" the others cry.

With open mouth he chews his food
A nasty sight and very rude!

Messy Bear

Messy Bear is smeared with honey

A sight that really is not funny.

If bears are careful how they eat

Then every meal can be a treat.

Please Bear

Please Bear thinks what a special day

Now all his friends have come to play.

"Maybe we will have some races?

But first let's wash our hands and faces."

Yelling Bear

Yelling Bear begins to scream

She's not been chosen for the team.

The other bears just look away

Far better to keep quiet and play.

Moaning Bear

"I want some cake!" says Moaning Bear

"To make me wait just isn't fair"

"It's already far too late!"

But good things come to those who wait...

Happy Bears

The birthday cake is a magic sight

When Mummy Bear turns off the light.

"Happy Birthday," they sing and shout

As Please Bear blows his candles out.

Soon the room is filled with laughter

The Bears are happy...Ever after!

Daily Mail's *'You Magazine'*
Book of the Week

Nice Bear Naughty Bear

Daily Mail
BOOK OF
THE WEEK
You Magazine

THE GOOD MANNERS BOOK

ISBN: 978-1-84886-039-1

"Both fun and fruitful, this enchanting Good Manners Book might help a few grown-ups too..."

Sarah Stacey, *You Magazine*